An Angel for Solomon Singer

Story by CYNTHIA RYLANT

Paintings by PETER CATALANOTTO

ORCHARD BOOKS · NEW YORK

Solomon Singer lived in a hotel for men near the corner of Columbus Avenue and Eighty-fifth Street in New York City, and he did not like it. The hotel had none of the things he loved.

His room had no balcony (he dreamed of beautiful balconies). It had no fireplace (and he knew he would surely think better sitting before a fireplace). It had no porch swing for napping and no picture window for watching the birds.

He could not have a cat. He could not have a dog. He could not even paint his walls a different color and, oh, what a difference a yellow wall or a purple wall would have made!

It is important to love where you live, and
Solomon Singer loved where he lived not at all, and
it was this that drove him out into the street each
night. It was dreams of balconies and purple walls
that took him to the street.

Solomon Singer wandered.

He was a wanderer by nature, anyway. He had grown up in Indiana, a place absolutely famous for wandering. So much of Indiana was mixed into his blood that even now, fifty-odd years later, he could not give up being a boy in Indiana and at

night he journeyed the streets, wishing they were fields, gazed at lighted windows, wishing they were stars, and listened to the voices of all who passed, wishing for the conversations of crickets.

Solomon Singer was lonely and had no one to love and not even a place to love, and this was hard for him. He didn't feel happy as he wandered.

One evening, somewhere between Columbus
Avenue and Central Park West, Solomon Singer
wandered into a small restaurant called the Westway
Cafe. He liked the name. He was from the Midwest
and liked to imagine he was, each day, making his way
west, that someday he would again be west, and so
the name meant something to him.

He opened up the plastic menu before him and
there he read these words: *The Westway Cafe—where
all your dreams come true.* The menu told him how much
hamburgers and bowls of soup and pieces of pie and
other things cost. But it didn't put a price on dreams.

A voice quiet like Indiana pines in November said,
"Good evening, sir," and Solomon Singer looked up
into a pair of brown eyes that were lined at the corners
from a life of smiling. Solomon Singer smiled back at
the waiter and ordered a bowl of tomato soup, a cup of
coffee, and a balcony (but he didn't say the balcony
out loud).

The tomato soup was delicious, and he even got a second
cup of coffee free, and the smiling-eyed waiter told Solomon
Singer to come back again to the Westway Cafe. Solomon
Singer did, the very next night.

He ordered two biscuits and some bacon and a large glass of grapefruit juice and a fireplace (but he didn't say the fireplace out loud). The smiling-eyed waiter was glad to see him, glad to have him, and told him, "Come back again," and Solomon Singer did, the very next night.

For many, many nights Solomon Singer made his way
west, carrying a dream in his head, each night ordering it up
with his supper. When he reached the end of his list of
dreams (the end was a purple wall), he simply started all over
again and ordered up a balcony (but he didn't say the balcony
out loud).

And slowly and quietly with time, something happened.
On Solomon Singer's walks each night to the Westway Cafe,
the streets began to move before him like fields of wheat, and
he thought them beautiful.

The lights in the buildings twinkled and shone like stars, and he thought them lovely. And the voices of all who passed sounded like the conversations of friendly crickets, and he felt friendly toward them.

Rounding the corner off Columbus Avenue, seeing the lighted window of the Westway Cafe, Solomon Singer felt as he had as a boy, rounding the bend in Indiana and seeing the yellow lights of the house where he lived.

Walking into the Westway Cafe, he felt at home as he had in Indiana, and the smiling waiter greeted him as familiarly as his parents had once greeted him in Indiana, when he would come in from wandering the roads he loved.

The waiter's name, it turned out, was Angel.

Solomon Singer went to the Westway Cafe every night for dinner that first year and he dines there still. He hasn't given up carrying a dream in his head each time he goes, and one of his dreams has even come true (he has sneaked a cat into his hotel room).

Solomon Singer has found a place he loves and he doesn't feel lonely anymore, and if ever you are near the Westway Cafe, wishing instead you were in a field of conversational crickets beneath the shining stars, go inside, and Angel will take your order and Solomon Singer will smile and make you feel you are home.

For Scott Rubsam . . . and for Angel—C.R.

For Paul—P.C.

Text copyright © 1992 by Cynthia Rylant. Illustrations copyright © 1992 by Peter Catalanotto. All rights reserved.
No part of this book may be reproduced or transmitted in any form or by any means, electronic or mechanical, including
photocopying, recording or by any information storage or retrieval system, without permission in writing from the
Publisher. Orchard Books, 387 Park Avenue South, New York, NY 10016. Manufactured in the United States of America.
Printed by General Offset Company, Inc. Bound by Horowitz/Rae. Book design by Mina Greenstein. The text of this book
is set in 16 pt. Plantin. The illustrations are watercolor paintings reproduced in full color.   10 9 8 7 6 5 4 3 2 1

Library of Congress Cataloging-in-Publication Data. Rylant, Cynthia. An angel for Solomon Singer / story by Cynthia
Rylant ; paintings by Peter Catalanotto.   p.   cm. "A Richard Jackson book." Summary: A lonely New York City resident
finds companionship and good cheer at the Westway Cafe where dreams come true.   ISBN 0-531-05978-2
ISBN 0-531-08578-3 (lib. bdg.)   [1. Loneliness—Fiction.   2. Wishes—Fiction.   3. Restaurants, lunch rooms, etc.—Fiction.
4. New York (N.Y.)—Fiction.]   I. Catalanotto, Peter, ill.   II. Title.   PZ7.R982An   1992   [E]—dc20   91-15957